Noah's Swim-a-Thon

Ann D. Koffsky

URJ PRESS
New York, New York
URJBooksandMusic.com

For all the kids at Ruach Day Camp who are brave enough to take the plunge! And for my *gibor chayil*, Mark, and my three fish, Aaron, Jeremy, and Adira.

Swim-a-Thon® is a registered trademark owned by USA Swimming. Used with permission.
Make a Splash is a national child-focused water safety initiative created by the USA Swimming Foundation, with the goal of teaching every child in America how to swim.
For more information, visit makeasplash.org.

Library of Congress Cataloging-in-Publication Data

Koffsky, Ann D.
  Noah's swim-a-thon / by Ann Koffsky.
    p. cm.
    ISBN 978-0-8074-1168-1
  [1. Camps--Fiction. 2. Swimming--Fiction. 3. Charity--Fiction. 4. Jews--United States--Fiction.]
I. Title.
  PZ7.K81935No 2010
  [E]--dc22

                    2010045732

Designed by Michael J. Silber
This book is printed on acid-free paper
Copyright © 2011 by URJ Press
Manufactured in Canada

10 9 8 7 6 5 4 3 2 1

Noah loved camp.

He loved kickball.

He loved painting
in arts and crafts

and singing Shabbat
songs in music.

But Noah did not love the pool. The water made his arms feel goose-bumpy, his eyes feel stingy, and his nose feel stuffy.

His lifeguard would try to give Noah reasons to get in the water.

"Hey, Noah, put your face in the water and I'll give you a sticker!"

I already have plenty of stickers, thought Noah. That was not a good reason.

"Hey, Noah, blow bubbles like this and the fish will hear you!"

Silly. There were no fish in the pool. That was not a good reason either.

"Noah, do a superhero float and you'll be able to swim!"

Now why would I want to do that? wondered Noah. If I swim, my whole body will be wet. I'll feel goose-bumpy, stingy, and stuffy all at the same time. That was not a good reason—that was a BAD reason.

So every day, Noah was happy playing kickball,
happy painting projects, and happy singing songs.

But he was very unhappy from the time he had to put on his bathing suit to the time he could put his clothes back on again.

Then one day, there was a big sign hanging on the wall in the lunchroom: "SWIM-A-THON IN TWO WEEKS!"

All of Noah's friends started talking when they saw the sign.

"What's a swim-a-thon?"

"Are we going to swim in the lunchroom?"

"Maybe they'll fill a big tank with the green bug juice and we'll swim in that."

One of the bigger kids at the next table heard them.

"We're not swimming in bug juice," she snorted. "I was here last year. You swim in the pool and you get a prize."

Prizes are good reasons, thought Noah. But not good enough to get me to swim!

Just then, Mrs. Rubin, the camp director,
stood in front of the lunchroom to speak.

"Shalom, campers!" she called over the microphone.

"Shalom!" they all answered together.

"Let me tell you all about the swim-a-thon. In a swim-a-thon, you can win wonderful prizes for swimming!"

All the campers cheered. Except for Noah.

"There are also prizes that you will be GIVING!"
Noah and his friends looked at each other, confused.

"There are many children who can't afford to come
to a wonderful camp like this one," Mrs. Rubin
explained. "They don't get to play kickball, make arts and
crafts, and sing Shabbat songs in music like you do."

No kickball? That sounded terrible to Noah.

"By swimming in the swim-a-thon, you will be giving those children a prize. You will be helping to send some of them to our camp." Mrs. Rubin explained that for every lap they swam, their friends and relatives would give a little money to the "Help Kids Get to Camp" *tzedakah* fund. Then Mrs. Rubin showed them all the great prizes that they would get for doing the swim-a-thon, and the kids started cheering again.

That night, when Noah was hanging his dry bathing suit and towel up, the swim-a-thon flier fell from his camp bag onto the floor.

His Mom picked it up. "Hey Noah, what's this?"

Noah told her all about the swim-a-thon, the prizes, and the *tzedakah* for the kids who couldn't go to camp.

"Are you going to do it?" she asked.

"I'm not sure. Swimming makes me feel goose-bumpy, and the prizes aren't such a good reason to feel goose-bumpy."

"That's true. The prizes aren't a good enough reason," his mom agreed.

"But maybe, y'know, the kids and the *tzedakah* might be a good enough reason," Noah said softly.

His mom smiled and handed Noah a book and the telephone.

"Here. This book has the phone numbers of Bubbe, Zayde, Cousin Max, Aunt Adina—all our relatives. Why don't you give them each a call, and see if you can fill out the pledge sheet?"

Noah called them all.

"Cool, dude. I'll pledge $1.
Don't sink, man."

"Put me and Zayde down
for $2 each, sweetie!"

"OK. Put me down for 75 cents, honey."

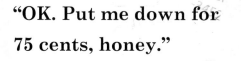

"Sure, kiddo! I'll give you $5 for every lap you swim!"

"Noah, what a wonderful *tzedakah*. I'd love to pledge $2. Good luck with it!"

When he was done, Noah sat down with his dad, and together they added up all the pledges he had gotten.

Swim-A-Thon Pledge Sheet

Swimmer Name: NoAH

Sponsor Name	$ per lap
CousiN ELi
CousiN JAY	$5
Uncle JUDAH	$1
AunT Lizzie	$2
Bubbe	$.75
Cousin SuE	$2
Mr. AAron	$.75
GrandmA Lynn	$2
Rabbi Diamond	$1
Uncle J.D.
AunT Rose
Mommy+Daddy
Mr. Goldberg

Total Per Lap:

They figured out that if Noah swam even one lap, twenty-five dollars would go to *tzedakah*!

At swim the next day, Noah
sat on the side of the pool.
His lifeguard came over.
 "Put your face in, Noah.
I'll give you a sticker."
 Noah was about to say no, like
he always did. Then he thought about
the kids who never got to paint camp
projects and the pledges he had gotten
last night. Noah took a deep breath and

SPLASH!

"All right, Noah!" said his lifeguard.
"One sticker for you!"

At swim the day after that, Noah put his face in right away.

His lifeguard came over again. "Let's see you blow bubbles and talk to the fish!"

There are no fish; it's a pool, not an ocean, thought Noah, and he almost said no again. Then he thought about the kids who didn't get to kick home runs in camp kickball.

Noah started blowing bubbles.

"Good job! Keep talking to those fish," his lifeguard smiled.

When he came to the pool the day after that, Noah got right in the water and blew bubbles.

"OK, Noah, I'm going to hold you so you can do a superhero float," his lifeguard announced.

Uh-oh, thought Noah. If I float, my whole body will be in the water— I'll feel goose-bumpy, stingy, and stuffy!

Then he remembered the kids who never got to giggle at a funny camp song.

"OK. Up, up, and away!" his lifeguard called. Noah put his whole body in and floated on top of the water. Hey, thought Noah, floating feels like flying.

For the next two weeks, Noah came to the pool each day and got his whole body in. He practiced floating over and over. Noah also started to move his arms and kick his feet, which made the floating turn into swimming.

(Sometimes in the pool Noah still felt goose-bumpy, stingy, and stuffy. But most of the time he felt like a flying superhero!)

Finally, swim-a-thon day came. That day Noah
was happy at kickball, arts and crafts, and music.

When it came time to put on his bathing suit,
Noah was happy then, too.

At the pool, all the lifeguards announced,
"Swim-a-thoners! On your mark, get set, go!"
They blew their whistles,
and everyone jumped in.

Noah jumped right in, too. He put his face in, blew bubbles, and kicked his feet!

His lifeguard started to cheer and clap just for Noah!

"Attaboy, Noah! Keep swimming!"

Noah swam. He kept swimming. Soon he was passing the ladder. Then he was halfway across the pool. The whole camp started to cheer just for him.

"No-ah, No-ah, No-ah!"
Even Mrs. Rubin was cheering!

When the lifeguards blew their whistles to end the swim-a-thon, Noah's fingers had just touched the wall of the pool—he had swum a lap!

The *tzedakah* fund would get twenty-five dollars because of his swimming.

Noah's lifeguard ran over to him.

"Noah, that was AMAZING! What made you decide to become such a happy swimmer?"

"I just needed a good reason," answered Noah. "But . . . I'll take that prize, too, if you have one!"